HORRENDO'S CURSE

ANNA FIENBERG

ART BY
RÉMY SIMARD

ADAPTED BY ALISON KOOISTRA

FOR STEFANO WITH LOVE—A.F.
TO BENOIT C.—R.S.

© 2013 Anna Fienberg (text)
© 2013 Rémy Simard/i2iart.com (illustrations)

Graphic novel adaptation by Alison Kooistra
Based on the novel *Horrendo's Curse*, © 2002 Anna Fienberg
Cover design by Natalie Olsen, Kisscut Design

Annick Press Ltd.

We acknowledge the support of the Canada Council for the Arts, the Ontario Arts Council, and the Government of Canada through the Canada Book Fund (CBF) for our publishing activities.

**ONTARIO ARTS COUNCIL
CONSEIL DES ARTS DE L'ONTARIO**

50 YEARS OF ONTARIO GOVERNMENT SUPPORT OF THE ARTS
50 ANS DE SOUTIEN DU GOUVERNEMENT DE L'ONTARIO AUX ARTS

Cataloging in Publication

Kooistra, Alison, 1979-
     Horrendo's curse : the graphic novel / Anna Fienberg ; art by Rémy Simard ; adapted by Alison Kooistra.

Also issued in electronic format.
ISBN 978-1-55451-549-3 (bound).—ISBN 978-1-55451-548-6 (pbk.)

     1. Fienberg, Anna. Horrendo's curse. 2. Graphic novels.
I. Simard, Rémy II. Title.

PN6733.K65H67 2013   j741.5'971   C2013-901251-6

Printed in China

Published in the U.S.A.
by Annick Press (U.S.) Ltd.

Distributed in Canada by
Firefly Books Ltd.
50 Staples Avenue, Unit 1
Richmond Hill, ON
L4B 0A7

Distributed in the U.S.A. by
Firefly Books (U.S.) Inc.
P.O. Box 1338
Ellicott Station
Buffalo, NY 14205

Visit us at: **www.annickpress.com**
Visit Rémy Simard at: **www.remysimard.com**

THE TWELFTH YEAR OF A BOY'S LIFE IS THE WORST.

HURRY UP, YOU SNIVELING SLOWPOKE!

I WOULD LIKE— IF IT WOULDN'T BE TOO MUCH TROUBLE—

I WISH THAT THIS YEAR, THE PIRATES WOULDN'T COME.

YOU CAN'T STOP THE PIRATES, NIMWIT!

YOU MIGHT AS WELL TRY TO STOP YOUR OWN SHADOW.

THE TWELFTH YEAR OF A BOY'S LIFE IS THE WORST.

BECAUSE IT IS VERY LIKELY TO BE HIS LAST.

1

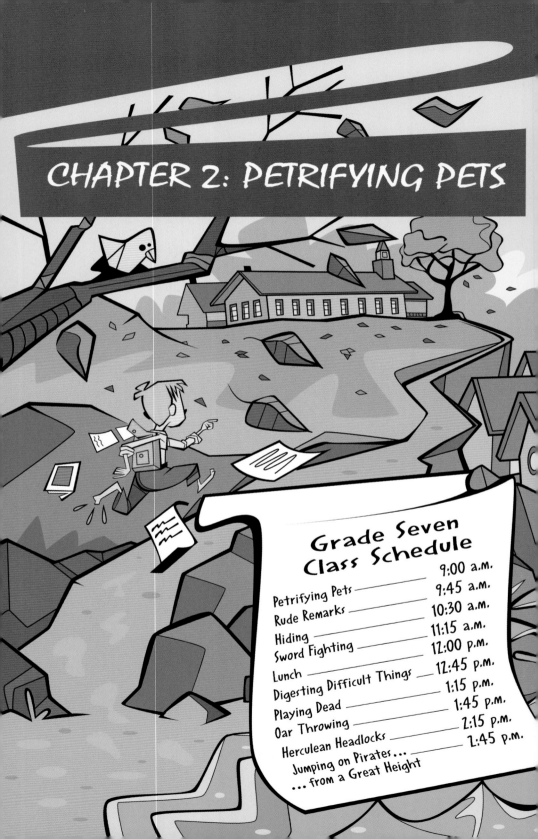

CHAPTER 2: PETRIFYING PETS

PEST ISN'T JUST A FROG! HE'S A POISON TONGUE FROG.

"HIS TONGUE IS LOADED WITH POWERFUL TOXINS. IF PEST SO MUCH AS LICKS YOUR LITTLE FINGER, YOUR BRAIN'LL SHRIVEL UP LIKE A LAND SLUG IN BRINE."

"FOR THE LAST FIVE MINUTES BEFORE YOU DIE, YOU'LL BE TORTURED BY TERRIFYING VISIONS. EVERY NIGHTMARE YOU'VE EVER HAD FLASHES BEFORE YOUR EYES."

"I'VE BEEN DOING EXPERIMENTS TO SEE IF I CAN INCREASE HIS LEVELS OF VENOM. I TRIED FEEDING HIM HEMLOCK LEAVES, BUT THAT JUST MADE HIM SICK."

"BUT PEST WON'T ATTACK UNLESS HE'S PROVOKED. HE MOSTLY USES HIS TONGUE TO CATCH BUGS."

SHUSH-SH-SH!! NOBODY ELSE CAN KNOW. THEY'D CALL ME A LILY-LIVERED FOOL.

AND DON'T GO THINKING WE'RE FRIENDS OR ANYTHING. WHEN WE GET BACK TO SCHOOL, DON'T ACT LIKE YOU KNOW ME.

OKAY, RASCAL.

WOULD YOU LIKE A SLICE OF BANANA BREAD?

YOU STINKIN'–

AHEM.

WHAT BOMBASTIC MEANS TO SAY, SIR, IS–

–WELL, IT'S JUST THAT WE HAVEN'T EATEN SINCE WE CAME ON BOARD.

THERE'S PLENTY FOR ALL OF US, SIR; I BAKED THIRTY LOAVES. I'VE ALSO GOT A POT OF SOUP GOING–IT'LL BE READY IN TIME FOR LUNCH.

YOU BOYS CAN HAVE THE OLD CATFISH AND JELLIED EELS IN THE KITCHEN.

WHAT ABOUT THE CAPTAIN, SIR? SHOULD I BRING HIM THE TRAY?

NO.

THE CAPTAIN WILL LIVE ON RUM AND SHIPS' BISCUITS LIKE HE'S ALWAYS DONE.

AND IF I WAS YOU, I WOULDN'T GO NEAR HIM 'LESS HE CALLED FOR ME.

AND EVEN THEN—

I—

ER—

OH NO—

BUUUR-UUURPP.

NOT THIS AGAIN, YOU SMELLY CARCASS! SHUT YER GOB OR TAKE YER BELLY-ACHIN' OVER TO THE STERN OF TH' SHIP!

DOES THIS HAPPEN A LOT, MR. DOGFISH, SIR?

AFTER EVERY MEAL. I GET THESE PAINS SHOOTIN' THROUGH ME.

YOU LAZY BUNCH OF SWINE, SLURPING OVER YOUR SWILL!

UMM ...

THERE'S A PIRATE SHIP COMING!

IT'S THE BLUE DEVILS!

WHAT!?!? WERE NONE OF YOU KEEPING WATCH?

BOOOOMMMM!!!!

NOW, YOU CRAVEN CHICKEN HEART, TELL ME WHERE YOU'VE STASHED YOUR TREASURE, OR I'LL BLAST YOUR SKULL TO SMITHEREENS.

IT'S— IT'S—

LIE TO ME AND YOU'LL PAY WITH YOUR LIFE. I KNOW IT'S SOMEWHERE IN THE SHIPWRECK ISLES.

AYE—THROUGH THE SCORPIO STRAIT—

THERE'S A VOLCANO—UP THE PATH— THERE'S A HUT—MARKED WITH A DEVIL'S HEAD—THAT'S—THAT'S WHERE—

OH—PLEASE— DON'T KILL ME ...

* HIC! *

I JUST WANT TO BURY IT THE RIGHT WAY. SAY GOODBYE AN' ALL.

MY LOYAL PINKIE, BEEN WITH ME ALL MY LIFE. IT PICKED MY NOSE WHEN ONLY A LITTLE FINGER WOULD DO—YOU KNOW THOSE HARD, CRUSTY BITS YOU GET UP THE BACK?

AND IT WAS ME DEAR PINKIE THAT WORE MAMMA'S RING.

I ALWAYS THOUGHT I'D PUT A GOLD HOOP THROUGH THAT EARLOBE, ONE DAY WHEN I GOT SOME TREASURE. BUT NOW ...

NOW THIS ... THIS IS THE POINT OF A MAN'S EXISTENCE.

OH, MR. BUZZARD, SIR, LOOK AT YOUR LEG! IT'S A WONDER YOU'RE STILL CONSCIOUS. I'LL JUST GO AND FIND SOME BANDAGES—

COULD YOU DO ANYTHIN' FOR AN EARLOBE?

HOW ABOUT MY POOR PINKIE?

I TOLD YOU TO SWAB THE DECKS AND KEEP A LOOKOUT! INSTEAD I FIND YOU HEN-BRAINED HACKS PECKING AT YOUR FEED AND CLUCKING YOUR TONGUES!

THE MEN ARE WOUNDED, SIR, AND PLEASE, SIR, I CAN SEE A CUT ON YOUR ARM, IF YOU WILL LET ME BANDAGE IT FOR YOU, I—

YOU!

NOW MARCH, BOY!

BEFORE I DIE, SIR, I'D LIKE TO GIVE MR. BUZZARD MY RECIPE FOR **LOBSTER** MORNAY.

JUMP, YOU DAWDLING DONKEY! *MORNAY.*

AAAAAAHHHHHHHH!!

THE WAVES ARE GOING TO SWAMP US!

THE PIRATES ARE GOING TO CATCH US!

WE'RE ALL GONNA DIE!

JUST RIDE THE WAVES WHEN THEY COME. DON'T WORRY— WE'LL FARE BETTER IN THIS SMALL BOAT GOING *WITH* THE SEA THAN THE PIRATES WILL FIGHTING IT IN THAT BIG SHIP.

AND IF WE ALL PULL TOGETHER, WE'LL GET TO SHORE IN NO TIME.

PULL TOGETHER IN A RHYTHM—

ONE,

TWO,

THREE,

ONE,

TWO,

THREE,

YOU'VE GOT IT! NOTHING CAN STOP US NOW.

ONE,

JABBERIN' JACKDAWS! I THINK THEY'RE TRYIN' TO TELL US SOMETHIN'.

FOLLOW THE DOLPHINS! THEY'RE GUIDING US TO SHORE!

NO WAY— WE'RE GONNA CRASH ON THOSE ROCKS!

SIZZLIN' STONEFISH—WE'RE RICH!

NOT SO FAST, YOU VERMINOUS VAGABONDS!

MOVE, BEFORE WE SLICE YOU OPEN LIKE A SCHOOL OF SARDINES!

WHY DON'T YOU ALL COME BACK AND LIVE IN OUR VILLAGE?

WHAT?!

WHY NOT? LET'S SAIL BACK AND SHARE OUT THE GOLD. YOU COULD ALL BUILD MANSIONS.

LIVIN' ON DRY LAND AND WAKIN' UP IN A WOMAN'S ARMS EACH MORNIN' ... I CAN JUST PICTURE IT.

PANCAKES EVERY DAY, AND NO MORE MOLDY FISH EGGS!

HOLD IT. WHAT'S IN THIS FOR US?

WHAT'S GOING ON?

WHAT DO THE PIRATES WANT FROM US NOW?

GREAT NEWS, EVERYONE! THE PIRATES AREN'T GOING TO HURT US ANY MORE—THEY ARE SETTLING DOWN HERE IN OUR VILLAGE! WE'RE GOING TO DIVIDE THIS TREASURE EQUALLY. AND—

NO.

EXCUSE ME?

I'VE CHANGED ME MIND. THIS 'ERE IS PIRATE GOLD, AND WE'RE NOT GOIN' TO SHARE IT WITH THESE SOFT-BELLIED LANDLUBBERS!

DON'T YOU DARE GIVE US ORDERS!

YOU KIDNAP OUR CHILDREN, YOU ROB US, AND YOU RUIN OUR LIVES!

RIGHT, RUINED—YOU HAD YER PICKET FENCES AND YER HOT DINNERS WHILE WE WAS SLAVIN' FOR THAT RUM-SODDEN DEVIL OF A CAPTAIN.

WE WERE YOUNG LADS ONCE, TOO, YOU KNOW— WE HAD HEARTS AND FEELINGS AND MOTHERS.

WHAT YER NEED TO UNDERSTAND IS—

ERG—

OH NO—

BUUR-URRR-UURRPP!!

OH, ME BELLY, IT'LL BE THE DEATH OF ME!

WOULD YOU— WOULD YOU LIKE SOME WATER?

I KNOW A REMEDY FOR INDIGESTION—I COULD BREW IT UP FOR YOU WITH HERBS FROM MY GARDEN.

THAT IS, IF YOU'RE PLANNING TO STAY FOR A WHILE.

AND SO, HORRENDO REFLECTED, THE SCUMMIEST CHAPTER IN LIFE'S ADVENTURES HAD TURNED OUT TO BE THE MOST SPLENDID.

HE THOUGHT ABOUT ALL THE PAIN OF THE PAST, AND ALL THE PROMISE OF THE FUTURE.

BLUSTA? I'VE BEEN WONDERING. DO YOU LIKE BANANA BREAD?

ONLY THE KIND WITHOUT COCKROACH PASTE.

THEN IT OCCURRED TO HIM THAT THERE WAS MORE TREASURE IN THIS MOMENT THAN ALL THE GOLD ON EARTH.

AND HE DIDN'T LET GO OF BLUSTA'S HAND, EVEN WHEN HIS OWN GREW ALL WARM AND SWEATY.

ABOUT THE AUTHOR AND ILLUSTRATOR

Anna Fienberg is an Australian author who has written many popular and award-winning books for children of all ages, including the *Tashi* series. *Horrendo's Curse* was first published as a novel, and it was an Honour Book in the 2003 Australian Children's Book Council awards.

Rémy Simard is a cartoonist, commercial artist, and award-winning author and illustrator. His work has appeared in a wide variety of magazines, newspapers, and books, including two nonfiction books published by Annick Press, *Duped!* and *Robbers!* He lives in Montreal, Quebec.

ALSO ILLUSTRATED BY RÉMY SIMARD:

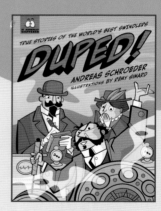

ROBBERS!
True Stories of the World's Most Notorious Thieves
by Andreas Schroeder
illustrated by Rémy Simard
paperback $12.95 • hardcover $21.95

"a fascinating and informative look at eight famous robbers and robberies around the world that will be enjoyed by many different readers. Highly recommended" —*CM Reviews*

DUPED!
True Stories of the World's Best Swindlers
by Andreas Schroeder
illustrated by Rémy Simard
paperback $12.95 • hardcover $21.95

"a fun lesson on how the masses can be made into fools." —*School Library Journal*
" it's hard to imagine a more kid-friendly piece of non-fiction." —*Booklist*